An Unknown Destination

SHALINI KUMAR

DEDICATION

Abhinav…my son.

CONTENTS

ACKNOWLEDGMENTS

A BIG thank you,

To Abhinav, for motivating, supporting, reading, listening
encouraging, trusting, criticising and shredding.

To Drishi, for her affectionate feedback.

To 'Family'- my furry stuffed companions - for their
unconditional love and support.

To my writing buddies for being all ears to my terrible first
drafts.

To Gingivitis, for checking on me from time to time.

Thank You!

For more mumblings and rumblings head to my website
www.flyhighopenbluesky.com

1 A LANDSCAPE AND A JOURNEY

Her bright smile and twinkling eyes, was what had attracted me to her kiosk, one of the many in that Art and Craft fair. I browse through the pile, mostly landscapes, hand painted, vibrant, eye catching. But it was one that caught my fancy.

'I'll buy this.'

Formalities over I walk out. A spring in my step.
Come evening I place it on my study table, sit back and admire. And am soon lost, transported to another world another time. What can I see? I ask myself.

I can see…
The mountains tall and imposing, a lake below, calm, placid its water, bottle green. Was it the reflection of the surrounding Sholas that made it look so? I can smell the mist, moist and feathery. I can hear the birds, rustle of leaves. I can see the winding paths, crisscrossing the mountain side. I can see the town, its houses with slanting roofs. I can see the small bazaar, stretched all the way downhill.

I squint a little, focus better, think harder…

I can see that toy shop dark and dingy. At the fag end of the market street. I can see the tiny car with blinking lights displayed in a rickety glass case. I can see you all of three, with a headful of curly soft hair. Looking dandy in your first pair of jeans. Pointing your plump finger I can hear you say 'yeh chahiye'! I can hear myself reply Phir se yeh! I can see your large eyes, wet and pleading. I can hear myself say, achcha le lo…I can see you run uphill flushed and excited whilst you clutch the white car close to your chest.

Amidst the same mountains I stand again. Many years later.

I can see the same bazaar, that toy shop, the lake, the Shola trees, the town, the houses with slanting roofs…but…I see something else…a school.

A final goodbye…

I can see you walk back inside, shoulders drooped unhappy.

I can see myself driving on without a backward glance.

I can feel your tears as I wipe mine.

Believe me, goodbye was as difficult for you as it was for me.

A hair pin bend and I can see the valley below.

Many such bends, I can see the vast plains ahead, dotted with windmills.

I am amazed at how much I can still see, and that the many intervening years have not dimmed my memory.

Picking it up gently I place it my drawer, to be seen some other day, some other time.

2 FOREVER JOY

Many years ago, these two, the protagonists, younger much younger, 35 and 11 respectively, on a trip to this quaint town tucked away in a far corner of that beautiful country…

On a wet cold day, done with sightseeing, he and she, walk the cobbled street. Cutting through the market, busy bustling vibrant inviting, they chance upon one, 'nik naks' it read. They decide to explore. And in no time, are lost in its wares, a collection of quirky and cute, handmade and unique. They browse and browse, through the maze, having forgotten their aching feet and numb hands.

He and she. Exploring row after row, shelf after shelf, wall hangings and roof danglers. They were transported to another world, mesmerising enchanting magical.

But, what caught her fancy was a low wood table, its smooth top holding the cutest and tiniest of glassware she had ever seen. Amongst them, was this, miniature tea set. Ceramic, hand painted, the entire set of 6 packed in a box, no bigger than her palm. An ardent lover of anything tiny, for her it was love at first sight. Aav dekha na taav, she picks it up and walks to the cash counter…

'5 pounds', she said tapping her machine.

'I won't be buying it just yet, thank you…'

Leaving it, they walk out…

'Mom why didn't you?'

'Will do it surely, sometime when the time is right…why waste now.'

Many many years passed since. Years full of traumas and turbulences, struggles and hard work.

It mattered no more or so she thought.

He unpacks his suitcase. His post grad is over.

'For you', he says as he places it on her palm.

'You remembered!'

'Of course how could I forget Mom?'

She hugs him. A bear hug.

Yes…it was a miniature tea set, ceramic hand painted a set of six, packed in a box, no bigger than her palm.

3 JEBKATRA (PICKPOCKET)

'Kyon be, phir jeb kaati'

'Ji sahab', he replies.

He picks up his *danda* and hits his butt. Bang on spot. Bullseye. Not an inch astray.

'Aage se jeb katega?'

'Nahin sahab, ma kasam', he replies rubbing his butt. And walks away. His gaze sharp, alert. On the lookout for his next target. His morning visit to the Lines has eaten into his precious few hours of work.

A seasoned jebkatra. *Danda* once in a while, would never deter him. To change his profession. Put his livelihood at stake. He was hardened and so was his butt. At having experienced the power of the *danda* many times a year.

Satisfied with the day's work, these two police inspectors decide to play a game of badminton. The court, in dire need of maintenance, adjoining the Police Lines. In this small town, somewhere in northern India.

Proceed to pull out rackets and a shuttle from a rickety wooden cupboard. Old and much used. Belonging to no one. Available for those, in the Lines, who happen to want to play.

They take their positions. On either side of the net. In police costume. Costume? Or Uniform? Costume, a reflection of their shabby, shaky and flabby policing.

It's a cold winter morning. Around 11 o'clock. The sun is bright and its warmth welcoming.

1st serve. The shuttle trembles, steadies, manages to cross the net. Just manages. The other runs, to hit, his heavy frame swaying in protest, misses, slips and falls.

Looking sheepish, gets up with a grunt dusts himself.

'*Yeh hamare liye nahin hai*', he decides as the other agrees. They walk back to the Lines. Pick up the well-oiled *danda*, 'yahi sahi hai' says one, giving a heavy blow to the black beetle crawling on the cracked floor.

Bang on spot. Not an inch astray.

4 PAPA'S ROSE

'*Kya ji bachchon ke samne kuch bhi*', chided Mummy, as we sat chatting, on our lawn, next to the fruit laden *Narangi*, midst a jungle of vibrant purple *Cineraria*, one winter morning. Enjoying our piping hot tea, three tea lovers, soaking in the warmth of the bright sun. The fourth, Abs was off to school.

I, back then, a 35 year old.

I still remember…

Papa and his half smile, when he teased Mummy.

'Papa how come you never had a girlfriend? How can that be?'

'Of course I had, beta. Rose, my Rose way back when I was in school'.

'*Kya Rose Rose laga rakha hai*' , interjected mom. '*Gulab thi beta, na ki Rose.*'

'Rose My Rose', sighed Papa dramatically.

Rose…

Standing in her *gauk*, every morning, waiting for him to cycle by.

Their houses in the same narrow lane in *Chchipitola.*

'Papa…who could've resisted?' I egged on.

'Right beta. Me, amiable, friendly, intelligent.'

'Mom you were lucky that papa said "Yes" to you.'

Yes for marriage to my mom, then 18 pursuing her under graduation. The first time he met her at her Baba's house in Meerut. A meeting arranged by elders.

'Yeh kya lucky the, mein koi Nutan se kam naa thi, upar se sughad aur samajhdar.'

'But, you could never be Rose, my Rose', continued Papa.

Mom gets up in a huff and walks away grumbling.

'Aapki zindagi bana di', her parting shot.

As corroborated by Papa's three siblings, Rose was not a fictitious character, a figment of his imagination. There was indeed a Rose, living down the same lane, a hopelessly in love Rose. Love…old time, never went beyond a few stolen glances, as she stood in her *gauk* and he cycled all the way to school.

5 AZIZ MASTERJI AND HIS BLUE CHALK

'*Kal se Aziz Masterji ayenge,*' announced mom one morning.

Unable to contain my excitement, I do a random dance, much to her surprise.

'*Unke aane se pehle tumhe itna khush kabhi nahi dekha.*'

For me, as an 8-year old, the very thought of getting another to add to my budding collection of colourful chalk, Aziz Masterji's blue chalk, was exciting enough. My big secret, which I had shared with none, not even mom.

Aziz Masterjii, the quintessential *darzi,* flowy orange beard, crochet *topi, crumpled kurta payjama, neel laga laga kar safed se zyada neela,* was a regular at our house, when we were young, young enough to happily don clothes, designed by our respective mothers and stitched by him. His visits lasted a few days at a stretch. His routine regimented, *toffan dhoop ya thandh,* started at 9 am sharp and ended by 5 pm.

Aziz Masterji, an integral part of our childhood. Our? Me, my sibling and cousins. Six in all.

Aziz Masterji, his requirements simple, specific, *haathwali silai machine, ek chatai, bhaithne ke liye saaf jagah, surahi ka paani, subah aur sham ki chai, multiple short breaks to smoke bidi* and gossip, a *pankha,* during summers. The *pankha,* on all his visits, happened to be the same, pedestal, faded green, noisy rickety.

Aziz Masterji a master craftsman, or so he thought. Trusted none, *kaatne se lekar button lagane tuk sub khud karte.*

His visit every time ended with mom saying

'Masterjiii ab silne ke liye kuch nahi hai.'

Collecting his payment, he would wave a cheery bye, *'phir milte hain'* and pedal away vigourously.

9 am next morning…

Alighting from his cycle, parking it carefully under the Guava tree, securely locking it, he proceeded to the garage, his abode or one can say his workplace for the next few days, gave a cursory glance, satisfied, took a deep breath, sat cross legged on the *chatai* and proceeded to empty the contents of his cloth bag, a tattered measuring tape, a pair of sharp metal scissors and blue chalk

It was that blue chalk I desired, square, plump in the middle and sharp on the edges.

'Namastey, Masterji!'

'Namastey, school ki chutti hai ka?'

'Haan Masterjee.'

'Kya chahiye? Gudiya ke kapde silwane hain?', smiling…

'Nahin Masterjii, pur kya ek chalk hum lelen.'

'Kahe?'

'Waise hi…'

'Abhi nahin sham ko jab kaam khatam ho jayega'.

A wee bit disappointed, I slowly climb the verandah stairs.

'Bhuliye ga nahin, Masterjii.'

'Chinta na karo.'

I was restless and spent the whole day keeping an eye on the clock ticking noisily, lethargically.

'Tumhare liye', he hands over a chalk to me as he winds up for the day.

'Thank you, Masterji', I shout happily, clutching it in my palm, I rush to where my box is hidden and gently drop it inside.

Back then how simple were the pleasures how simple was life!

6 AN ENCOUNTER IN THE LINES

'Tune phir jeb kaati?'

'Ji sahib.'

'Sudhrega nahin. Pichchlee bar ki maar bhool gaya?'

'Nahin sahab', rubbing his butt. *'Abhi bhi dukhat hai.'*

Picking up his danda ready to aim.

'Rukiye sahab. Yeh taraf nahin. Yeh taraf', putting his other butt forward. To take the hit.

'Sasura, bahut besharam hai.' He lets the *danda* fall on the floor.

'Agar jeb katani hai toh kat. Pakda kyon jaata hai be? Bar bar pitne ka shauk hai?'

'Nahin sahib.'

'Phir kyun?'

'Abhi training per hoon. Ustaad ki. Jab ustaad ban jaoonga, tub, aap humko kabhi nahin dekhoge.'

He smiles cheekily, flashing his tobacco stained black teeth.

'Hut chal bhaag saale. Phut. Gadha kahin ka.'

Humming, the jebkatra saunters out of the Lines, the Police Lines. Alert. On the lookout for his next prey.

7 THAT CHULHA

Our rendezvous that late winter evening, moonless and silent, happened to be the unkempt corner of our vast kitchen garden. Home to the mighty Guava, unruly *Caina, Anjeer,* puny veggie saplings, clumps of *Mogra* bushes, tiny *Nimboo* trees laden with *khatta* yellow fruit.

The surrounding darkness was broken by a dim, unsteady light from the solitary petromax, casting eerie shadows.

Behind us, stood our house bright, yet not enticing enough.

Squatting on the *medh* of the *Anjeer kyari*, braving the cold, our childish fears we, me and my cousin, still a few years away from our teens, wait.

Stoically ignoring the loud calls of our respective mothers…

'Kahan ho? Khana laga hai, Jaldi aao?'

What had attracted us to this part of the garden, that particular night?

Well!!!…it was the lure of the *chulha*. A temporary structure built of red bricks, placed to form a three sided square, liberally coated with a mix of smooth brown mud and *gobar*, stuffed with dry wood, twigs, paper.

In front of it sat Teejo, on the ground, swept and clean. Busy, very busy. Chopping, soaking, slicing, kneading, rolling grinding. Prep done, she proceeds to light the *chulha* with amazing dexterity and expertise. Stroking and fanning, till it turned into a roaring, hot dragon, smoke spewing hissing. Its flames twirling, dancing, flushing our faces, pricking our eyes.

On it she places an aluminum pot.

Watching, fidgeting but glued to our spot, we sit waiting, a trifle impatiently.

'Aur kitna time lagega, Teejo?'

'Sabar rakhen bhaiyya.'

Was her reply to our oft repeated question.

Sabar for us was running out fast.

What were we waiting for?

Teejo's dinner. Being cooked on that magical *chulha*, in a covered aluminium pot. Simmering, sizzling, bubbling.

Was it something exotic? For us it was! *Dul tukki*, yellow dal, small round thick rotis and a ball of freshly ground aromatic masala all tossed in.

But wasn't a lavish dinner waiting inside? It was, but not lavisher than this being cooked on the *chulha* that night.

They call us again, their tones edgy, irritated.

'Itna bulane par bhi kaan mein joon nahin reng rahi? Lagta hai pitai khane ka man hai!'

Teejo jumps to our rescue,

'Bhaiyya log humre saath khayenge, bibiji she replies loudly.

'Yeh bachche bhi! Khair, Teejo, tum andar se sabzi le lena, kabhi tumko khana kum na pade.'

'Kahe chinta karat hain bibiji. Jaise Radhey, Ghani vaise bhaiyya log. Kono phark nahi hai.'

She stirs at regular intervals, whilst we keep our vigil. Our tummies growling gnawing,our mouths watering.

'Ho gaya', she says as she places the pot on the ground with the help of two *Caina* leaves.

Doles out *karchul* full on an old dented *tashtari*, places it in front of us, to devour.

'Araam se khaiyyo kahin muh na jal jaye', she warns tenderly.

Teejo, our maid for many years, had temporarily shifted base, to our house for a month, a ritual she followed every year after year. Pitching in for Jagan who was away on an annual visit to his village.

She with her children, Radhe and Ghani. Packed her meager possessions in a *kathari,* locked her tiny mud hut on the outskirts and walked all the way to our house.

As always, she made that corner of our kitchen garden her kitchen. *Gobar se leep kar saaf safai karke, chulha banana mein jut gayi thi.* That day was her first.

We sat near the *chulha* gorging her delicious dinner as she walked inside, carrying a *pateela* to get *subzi* for her family. Our food, as much a treat for her, as hers was for us.

8 MISS GINGIVITIS, THE ROADARIAN AND HER PROMISE…

A recap-

'Mummy ka dhyan rakhna' *he had said, as he fed her for the last time, before he left his home to go to 'his' home. Both his. But kind of far apart. She had looked at him with large melting eyes, understanding his concern and in her tender heart, had made a promise.*

A year later.

'Gingi'

A fleeting glance, a quick wag, as she stands next to the *kuda wala,* her BFF, who is busy with his daily chore of collecting garbage from my neighbour's house.

'Gingi yahan aao.'

A jig, she stays put, her eyes fixated elsewhere.
Mystified, I follow her gaze. Targeting a squirrel,

nervous rushed, trying to hide behind the leaves of the scanty *Gurhal* bush, Madam Gingi is out to prey or play, difficult to say.

I try to distract her, but she remains focused, determined.

'Gingi!' I call out louder.

She shifts her gaze, giving that sliver of an opportunity to the hapless squirrel to escape.

Having lost her, she finally turns to me. Tail wagging, dancing the Gingi dance, she trots up to me.

'Itne din kahan thi?'

Its early morning. Pleasant and cool. The last few months of frigid cold have finally given way to spring. Still in my night clothes with a light jacket thrown in, I had walked out of the main door, proceeded to unlock the side gate and happened to peep out. And whom do I see?

My Gingi, after many no-show days. Of course, her nightly visits and vigil continue, near the *Amaltas*, tall and imposing, nude and leafless, where the main road meets the narrow lane. I recognise her bark, distinctive from others, She comes without fail. But her daytime visits are intermittent, sporadic.

'Kaisi ho?'

Her expressive eyes convey all.

I bend to pat. *'Ruko pedigree laati hoon.'*

She shows little interest.

Time to accept that my Gingi is no longer that little girl, she used to be. She is all grown up and mature. Capable of fending for herself.

I turn to walk inside, but not before looking back and saying,

'*Gingi, tum itni jaldi badi kyun ho gayee.*'

Understanding my emotional state, she rushes to me and rubs her snout to my leg.

'*Aati rehna, bhoolna mut*', my parting shot.

She looks at me with her large melting eyes, as if to say, 'A promise for me is a promise for life.'

Yes, she is talking of the same solemn promise she had made that day, a year ago, a promise she has always kept.

9 HE FINDS A BRIDE

'Namastey Sahab'

Instinctively, his hands rush to *tatolo* his hip pocket. He smiles, relieved on feeling the bulge, of his black rexine wallet. The police inspector, usually manning the Lines, the Police Lines, in this small town, somewhere in Northern India, is not on duty. He's in Chowk, in the old part of town, buying vegetables.

'Kaisa hai be?' Teri dhwaja kuch badli si hai?'

'Theek, sahab' as he pulls a saree clad, *ghunghat kiye women.*

'Pair chchooo…'

She dutifully bends and touches his feet.

The inspector jumps back.

'Sahab, meri wife.'

Pulling the jebkatra aside, he whispers.

'Tu shaadi shuda hai be?'

'Ji, sahab.'

'Sasur ko kya bataya, saale?'

'Ji, bujiness hai.'

'Jhooth bola?'

'Ji jebkatre ko koi ladki kyun deta', he replies, looking serious.

'Kya naam hai?'

'Phoolvati'

'Bitiya lo', handing her a 20 rupee note.

'Rehne de sahab.'

'Tujhe nahi de raha.'

'Sahab jaldi milte hain.'

'Saala, harami moti chamdi hai, pure pichchwade par dande barsaaonga', mutters the inspector, as the jebkatra, walks away. Alert for his prey, as many could be found in this human infested market.

He needn't worry about Phool.

Her face was covered securely with a *ghoonghat*.

Ignorant, very ignorant, that Phool, his demure Phool,

was also adept, very adept, at picking pockets. Ladies' purses to be precise, tucked deep inside their blouses.

10 A TETE-A-TETE

…with me and my Lockdown Partners, my Notebooks.
From the point of view of…Navy and Orange

NAVY

I squint my eyes to decipher. Her scrawl. Atrocious!! How can a human write this bad? Is she one? A human? Scribbles with a pencil. Her ABCs incomprehensible. I have seen her spent hours trying to decipher hers.

Her forte? Twisting the ground rules. She believes in writing, frenzied and fast. Trying to keep pace with ideas, as they tumble out, topple one over the other. She wants to miss none.

Is she possessed? I don't think so, having had the privilege of observing her, closely, doing other chores. Organised and disciplined. Is it me? Maybe? Making her go crazy.

It can be any time of the day. When I am picked up. Browsed through. And the writing starts. At times lasting a few minutes or stretching to an hour. She writes, she smiles, as she visualises, her eyes at times wet, as she remembers, twinkling, when she achieves. Lost in her wonderland. Done. She shuts me. And sits still. Staring in space. An impromptu jig. Says all. I know she is elated. With what she just created.

Coming back to me, today is my superannuation. For the ignorant. My retirement. Full to the brim. I am all set to be added to the pile of three…Red, Yellow, Pink and me, Navy blue. But how can she let go…without her trademark taunt 'I never wrote my best with you. I hope the next, gives me better stories.' It breaks my heart. Others in the pile have similar stories to narrate.

Before I bid bye, a little something about my replacement. Loud, ostentatious and boisterous. Orange. A bright Orange. When will she grow up? She should mellow with age. But who dare advise her. Not me, Just retired and already on pension.

11 ORANGE

I am 'Orange', bright, eye catching.

Freshly out of quarantine spent in a white plastic basket, sitting atop the shoe rack. Waiting and waiting and waiting, for this torture to end.

'10 days'…she had said with finality.

Maybe, a miracle! I was proven wrong.

Each night I mentally ticked off a day from my calendar of 10.

As for her, she kept a safe distance.

11th day…

She roughly rips my plastic shield, does a quick recce and plonks me on her study table not hers but won over in a battle of sorts.

I look around. What a mess! Stacks of paper, random

books, a sharpener, writing tools. But it is the 'Pile' that catches my attention. Occupying the far corner, sitting sedately, neatly, Red, Yellow, Pink, Navy. My twins, in different colours.

'Ah! companions finally' I mutter to myself as I approach them.

'Hi', I say cheerily.

'Hello,' 'they' reply gruffly.

'Orange' I introduce myself.

'We are not colour blind', 'their' cryptic reply.

'What a bunch of cynics!'

They unstack and examine, 'Me'.

Navy…

'New?'

'Yes, can't wait to start', I reply.

'They' whisper and snigger.

'What? Do share, consider me your own', I plead.

'Brute. Her tongue malicious, her taunts killing. She… hellish.'

'Scared?' they ask

'Yes' I reply, in trepidation.

'I was the first, and faced the worst of her outbursts'. says 'Red'.

'She is a hardened demon', says 'Yellow'.

'Be prepared for whacks and bumps curses and more curses. All the best!' pipes in 'Pink'.

'I was taunted down to an untimely death. Yet to recover from the onslaught', says 'Navy'.

Hear her approach, 'they' pile up at their assigned spot. She is touchy about spots. Maybe certain spots give her better stories.

She pushes her chair, roughly noisily, picks me up and warns,

'Give me nice stories or else' she threatens sounding ominous.

'I' shudder. She stares, unblinking cold piercing.

Our eyes meet, 'mine' scared uncertain and hers determined.

12 ORANGE AGAIN…

Scribbling ferociously, she stops, suddenly, sighs and sits back. 'No good' she mutters, winds up, retires for the night.

As for me…

Left alone, on the table, the one which she had won in a battle of sorts, the last of my ruled pages filled up, over, done with.

Lonely, sad, confused, I inch closer to…'them'.

'Them'…Red, Yellow Pink Navy, stacked in a pile, chatting and laughing.

Seeing me approach they fall silent…

A few seconds pass before Navy takes the initiative to break the ice, no friendly banter, no beating around the bush, just a few words of wisdom…

'Be prepared, mate, for the final shove, her trademark

taunt. Ruthless, soul ripping!' 'he' forewarns.

'Mmmmm' is all I can say, my somber dark mood, enveloping my very being.

Come morning…
She approaches the table, roughly pulls the chair, picks me up, stares, deeply frowning…

'You, gave me nothing. All show no depth.'

Clearing my throat…

'Wrong', I counter.

'Right', she needles me.

'Your fault not mine. Wallowing in self pity.'

'So?'

'So, why blame me, for non performance.'

'I will if I want to', she argues stubbornly albeit childishly.

'Your choice.'

'Yes, my choice. Who are you to dictate.'

'I am the NOTEBOOK.'

'So?'

Don't forget, the jebkatra, Battakh the duck, Ullooo and his Owlets, etc, etc. conceived, scribbled revised, rescribbled rerevised re rescribbled, rerere'…I pause to catch my breath, '…on me'.

'That was me writing brilliantly.'

'Oh! Come on. Look beyond I, Me, Myself.'

Her lips pursed, or I can say cruelly curled, she pushes me, at the very bottom of the pile.

Picks up Black, a visibly shivering black, unnerved, unsettled shaken, having witnessed the bitterest of arguments.

'Congrats, man, you surely gave it back', 'they' thump my back.

As for me, too young to retire, I get busy.

Copying ferociously, from her million scribbles to create my own book.

Starry eyed, I Dream. BIG, real BIG…

This year's Best Copier Award goes to Orange…for his book titled…

'Scribbles & Dribbles

Tickles & Giggles'…

A brightly lit stage and deafening applause…as I trot up beaming, to collect my award, waving cheerily at a smiling 'them' Red, Yellow, Pink, Navy, Black and a scowling 'her'.

13. A DRESSING DOWN

'Agla!'

Calls out the inspector, the same police inspector, manning the same Police Lines that winter morning, in the same small town, somewhere in Northern India.

Spectacled, noting furiously…

'Naam?'

'Balam.'

'Poora naam?'

'Ram Balak.'

'Pita ka naam?'

'Ram Nihore.'

'Mata ka naam?'

'Kaushalya.'

'Naam pavitra aur kaam…apavitra,' he mutters.

'Umar?'

'Pachees.'

'Galat kaam?'

'Jeb kaati.'

The inspector looks up, squints, stares, recognises

'Phir? Tu? Shadi ke baad bhi? Pit pit kar karer ho gaya hai be!'

Instructing his havaldar…

'Iske pichchwade par intne barsa ki salaa jeb kaatna bhool jaye…'

Flashing his tobacco stained teeth, rubbing his butt, he walks, to the veranda, to get his share of the beating…

Havaldar lifts his danda…

'Sahab kha lo', he whisks out a *paan*.

'Maghai?'

'Ji sahab.'

'Surti, kaththa, chuna, supari?'

'Bhar ke…'

Stuffing it in deep inside his wide mouth…

'*Chal bhag*'…he whispers, hitting the floor hard with his danda as the jebkatra groans loudly…

'*Are bas kar*', shouts the inspector from inside the Lines. '*Jaane de waarning de kar…*'

Havaldar ka paan havaldar ko khilaker, the daring jebkatra saunters out of the Lines, alert, on the lookout.

Calling out to Phool, his *Phool si phool, ghoonghat mein chchcipi Phool,* sitting outside the Lines under a *Sehjan,* waiting for him.

'*Chal, tujhe aaj Katra ghumata hoon.*'

'*Awat hoon*', she replies softly.

She adjusts her *ghoonghat,* alert, careful not to lose sight of her next target, yet another *koodhmagaz auratiya* with money tucked in the deep confines of her blouse.

14 BATTAKH, THE DUCK

Somewhere in the vast plains of Northern India was this pond, misshapen, secluded. But then aren't there innumerable dotting the vast flat terrain? Yes, but this one was special. It housed three ducks. Battakh, the duck, was a novelty in this part of the country.

Life was idyllic for these three, white with bright yellow beaks and orange webbed feet.

Near this pond traversed a narrow tarred road, rough, uneven, unused at least by motorists. Branching out of a highway heading to some village or a *kasba*.

That afternoon was like any other. Cool and calm except for a slight breeze.

Till…

A black bulky vehicle full of humans screeches to a halt. They spill out and start mapping.

'Khana yahin pe khayenge.'

As for the children, untethered they set out to explore. Poking prying, running shouting, a riotous bunch.

The three ducks, alarmed by this sudden invasion, decide to take refuge amidst the weediest part of the pond. Feeling safe they breathe easy but, a wee bit too early.

'*Papa? Dekho!*' shouts a lad, thin, short, dark, upon spotting them half hidden amongst the tall weeds.

'*Kya be, Tillu?*' asks his father, coming nearer.

'*Battakh*', points Tillu.

'*Phaltu mein bulaya battakh dikhane ko.*'

Not one to give up, '*chalo pakde!*' shouts Tillu as the other kids join in and manage to get hold of one after a ferocious struggle.

Tillu carries Battakh, by now comatose with shock, up to where his granny is busy boiling water in a *bhagona* to prepare tea.

'*Isme daal doon?*', he asks, ready to dunk Battakh in the *bhagona.*

'*Hut, pagal*', chides his granny. '*Chal chchod de?*' she directs authoritatively.

Tillu reluctantly lets go of the hapless Battakh. Too shocked to fly, he walks a few unsteady steps, recovers his wits and rushes to the pond. Jumping in and swimming at breakneck speed, he stops only after reaching the other end where his mates are paralysed by what's transpiring before them.

He snuggles up, relieved, having just suffered a near death experience of being boiled alive in a *bhagona*. Learnt a life lesson, to stay clear of humans, particularly the little ones. Only grannies could be trusted. God bless that Granny!

Coming back to the grass patch.

'*Papa?*' calls out Tillu yet again.

'*Dekho kauvva. Usko pakde?*'

'*Are hut be gadhe*', says his papa, angry at having been disturbed while enjoying his sumptuous lunch.

Kids gear up to catch the *kauvva*.

'*Lagta hai police banega sasura, har samay kisi na kisi ko pakadne ke liye peechche bhagna*', says papa proudly.

15 AFTEREFFECTS OF LOCKDOWN

Under the *Sehjan* tree, one afternoon…

'Kyun be? Kaisa hai? Bahut dino se nahin dhikha?'

'Sahab, lockdown ne toh mera bujiness khatam kar diya. Sub ghar mein jo ghuse the!'

'Aur tu?'

'Mein bhi.'

Taking off his mask, he smiles cheekily and continues…

'Sahab, jaldi milte hain, Lines mein', and quick as lightning alights an e-rickshaw and is soon lost.

'Sasura kabhi sudhrega nahin', the inspector smiles fondly, as he saunters back to the Lines, the Police Lines in that small town somewhere in Northern India.

16 PHOOLWATI

'Phool, chal thodi taazi hawa kha kar aate hain!', says the jebkatra to his wife, Phool, that summer evening.

Phool, sans her *ghoonghat* looked different. Draped in a bright pink floral saree, clipped firmly at her shoulder and near her navel, with stone studded clips, seemed urbane, polished. Slipping her alta painted feet into high heel chappals,

'Taiyyar hoon!'

They saunter out onto the street in front of their house.

Does she know about him? And him of her?

Strolling down the pavement, hand in hand, laughing and chatting, these two seem in perfect sync.

'Are ruk!' he hails, the black and yellow *phatphatiya*, crammed with people halts with an audible creak.

'Chowk chalega?'

They alight, their faces transformed to taut focused alertness.

While she settles amongst the women and he with the men, the p*hatphatiya* revs with a jerk and is soon lost leaving a cloud of dust and a trail of acrid black smoke.

As for the passengers, *bilkul anjaan ki chowk pahunchne tuk unka batua unki jeb mein hoga ya kisi aur ki!*

THE END.